I0734484

MARY CRAWFORD

Dreams Change

HIDDEN BEAUTY NOVELLA 3

COPYRIGHT

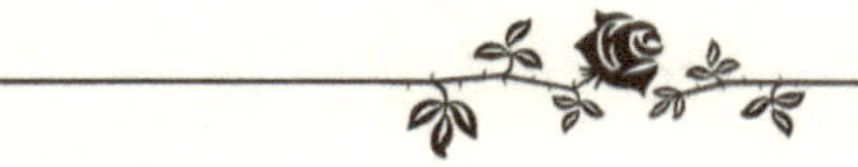

HIDDEN BEAUTY SERIES

Until the Stars Fall from the Sky

So the Heart Can Dance

Joy and Tiers

Love Naturally

Love Seasoned

Love Claimed

If You Knew Me (and other silent musings) (novella)

Jude's Song

The Price of Freedom (novella)

Paths Not Taken

Dreams Change (novella)

Heart Wish (100% charity release)

Tempting Fate

The Letter

The Power of Will

Hidden Hearts Series

Identity of the Heart

Sheltered Hearts

Hearts of Jade

Port in the Storm (novella)

Love is More Than Skin Deep

Tough

Rectify

Pieces (a crossover novel)

Hearts Set Free

Freedom (a crossover novel)

The Long Road to Love (novella)

Love and Injustice (Protection Unit)

Out of Thin Air (Protection Unit)

Soul Scars (Protection Unit)

OTHER WORKS:

The Power of Dictation

Use Your Voice

An Everyday Guide to Scrivener 3 for Mac

Vision of the Heart

Dedication

To parents everywhere
who love and accept
their children
regardless of how
they arrive.

Thank you.

Chapter One

Tara

I MUST BE A glutton for punishment. Why else would I schedule myself to teach a Mommy-n-Me ballet class? I could've passed it on to one of my senior dance students who are always clamoring to work in the studio to earn teaching time. For some reason, I didn't. Now I am about to shatter into a thousand pieces over the acoustic version of *Twinkle, Twinkle Little Star.*

There was a time in my life when I was exceptionally good at walling off emotion and pretending I didn't care. I've almost forgotten who that woman is. She is gone — replaced by someone who has all the love and support she would ever need. So … why do I feel so alone?

Aidan has tried to be there to fill the void. Yet, I am beginning to fear I'll have a hole in my soul until the day I die. The distance between Aidan and I seems to be growing larger every day and I don't know how to stop it. Aidan thinks we can talk through it like we do everything else in our marriage. I have my doubts. This is different.

Whenever we try to talk about 'that day' I become totally numb inside. Actually, there have been several days like "that day' over the past few years, but the most recent one was the worst yet. These days, I can't even force myself to look at a calendar. I can't forget. If things had gone the way they were supposed to, I would be holding Adriana in my arms in a couple of weeks.

Things did not go right. They went as wrong as anything can go. I will never forget that day for as long as I live. I wish I could, but it's just not possible. It will haunt me forever.

Things should have been perfect — all the scans and tests said so. Yet, somehow, they weren't.

Given my recurrent history of miscarriage, the OB/GYN was being extra careful. We all were. I did everything asked of me. This included painful shots every day and a complete, radical overhaul of my daily life. I was okay with the sacrifices because being a mother was worth it.

I had just gone to the doctor three days before 'that day'. Dr. Worthington examined me and Adriana's ultrasound and pronounced everything to be as expected and there was nothing to be concerned about. She told me to wait a week and then stop the hormone shots. I didn't make it a full week before Adriana was gone.

It was a typical day. Aidan was scheduled to give a big concert and he had special guests coming. We met them in Tennessee when he and Tasha were at St. Jude's Hospital. While Aidan worked on a few changes to his playlist, I was online doing a little baby shopping. After all, I was three days from the end of my first trimester.

Aidan was joking with me. He said if I kept spending money, he would have to take a second job. He volunteered to practice his masseuse skills on me to show me it was entirely possible for him to make a supplemental income on the side. Of course, this was ridiculous because Aidan's album had gone triple platinum in a week and a half. I could buy several baby boutiques on the royalties alone.

My nausea had eased to a tolerable level, and I was feeling good. I remember thinking to myself, '*It's a great time to be me. I love my life.*' I had barely finished that thought when I felt something pop and felt a warm gush of liquid between my legs.

I wish I could tell you I thought I had simply peed myself, but I can't. I knew in an instant Adriana was gone.

As soon as Aidan heard my guttural cry, he sprang into action. He yelled for the rest of the crew to call 911 and carried me downstairs as blood was soaking into my leggings. He was more panicked than I've ever seen him as he demanded the ambulance take me to the nearest hospital with lights and sirens. I broke down when I heard him say it because Aidan and I have reached the level of fame where anything we do is no longer anonymous — everything is reported in the tabloids and most of it makes national news. I didn't want my grief to be displayed to the public.

Fortunately, there were other people in the house who could calm Aidan down enough so he was able to think things through. Aidan arranged for me to ride to the hospital with his new bodyguard, Nick. He and Logan took another vehicle in case the paparazzi were following us.

I know Aidan was hopeful something could be done to save Adriana. Sadly, I knew from the first moment — she was gone.

We waited for what seemed like forever in the ER. When I finally was placed in a private room, I completely lost it. I began to cry so hard I had difficulty breathing. My reaction was so severe my doctor decided to keep me for observation. Aidan and I have been married for eight years but we fell in love as teenagers. Because I'm over thirty five, we knew fertility treatments and pregnancy carried risks, but Adriana is the third pregnancy I've lost in eight years.

My private trip down memory lane is interrupted when I feel a tug on my skirt. "Miss Tara, why does our dancing make you so sad?" four-year-old Corrine asks me. Her lower lip, trembling. "I thought you liked it when we dance."

I bent over and fix Corrine's barrette which was about to fall out. "Your dancing is beautiful. I was just thinking about something else that made me sad."

"You told us dancing fixes things when you feel yucky. Maybe you should dance with us," she says as she pats me on the arm.

I remember a time when I did think dancing cured all the ills in the world. I know better now. Even so, Corinne's attempt to cheer me up makes me smile.

"You're right," I confirm with a watery grin. "I should take my own advice and dance away my troubles."

Corinne skips over to my karaoke machine. "I'm

too little to read, but I want you to play *Shake It Off*. That song always makes you smile."

"You're right again. My best friend, Kiera, has turned me into a Taylor Swift fan. That would be a fun song to dance to. Let me see if I can find it." I walk over to the office, take my phone out of my purse and put it on the docking station with the speakers. It only takes a couple of clicks and the catchy, sassy song kicks in.

I turn and face the class. "We've had a special request. Everyone do a silly dance."

A huge cheer comes up from the class. Silly dances are everyone's favorite. As I prepare to join the class, Aidan comes through the front door. "Cool beans! Was this class so spectacular they earned a silly dance? Do you need a partner?"

I look up at my beautiful husband with his goofy grin and sign, "Always."

Chapter Two

Aidan

I try not to cringe as I watch Tara pick through her food again. Even though I fixed her favorites, she seems uninterested in eating. It's been that way for months. I'm concerned because Tara is already thin and she really can't afford to lose more weight.

"How was class today?" I ask, attempting to spur normal conversation, because the silence is deafening. I use sign language as I speak just in case Tara feels like communicating with her hands. It seems like our quirky, casual camaraderie has completely gone. Tara barely speaks to me now.

"I'm thinking about giving the Mommy-n-Me class up," she responds quietly.

"Why? Teaching the Littles has always been your favorite part of the day."

"Aidan, I can't do it anymore. I look at their sweet little faces and all I can think of is how it should have been me in a couple of years."

"I'm so sorry, Gracie," I respond, reverting to my childhood nickname for Tara.

"Are you really sorry?"

"Yes. Why would you even question that?"

"Well… it just seems you've been able to totally go on with your life as if nothing happened. Everything happened. Our whole life changed, but yours didn't. I feel like I'm the only one who misses Adriana."

My gut clenches. It feels like a well-placed roundhouse to my stomach. Can't she see my pain?

"That's just not true!"

"Oh yeah? Show me how your life has changed. You are still on tour with Tasha. You only took a month off. Do you expect me to get over this in a month?"

"No! I don't expect for you to get over it in a month, six months or six years."

"So, why aren't you as devastated as I am?"

"I don't think it would be possible for me to be as devastated as you. Adriana was part of you. That doesn't mean I wasn't destroyed by the loss." I struggle to find the words to express the sorrow which has taken up residence in my heart.

"Well, you could've fooled me. From where I sit, it looks like you think it's not much different than one of my panic attacks or headaches."

"I don't think you want me to tell you how I feel. It might hurt too much. There's a reason I keep my thoughts to myself. I'm trying to be supportive and not remind you of the trauma."

"AJ, you can't protect me from this. It happened to me. It's not like one of my blisters that you can put a Band-Aid over. You might as well tell me."

"Are you sure? It's pretty dark. I'm not even sure I can put all of it into words."

"Yes, I'm sure. Your thoughts can't be darker than my reality."

"I'm not so sure of that — but if it'll make you feel better, I'll share my experience."

"I think it will. Believing you don't care is excruciating. This has to be better."

"Okay, but don't say I didn't warn you. There isn't a day which goes by that I don't think of Adriana. I wonder if she could feel her life slipping away. Did she hear how much we loved her and then how much it hurt you when you started bleeding? I keep wondering if I should have canceled the tour the second I learned you were pregnant. I wonder whether I pushed you too hard to stay with me. If you had been on complete bed rest, would things have been different?"

"You blame me?" Tara whispers. She looks shattered. I hate that. It reminds me of how torn up she was by life back when we first reunited.

"No, I don't — we don't know what caused it this time or the last two. Maybe it's not you at all. It might be me because I had meningitis as a kid and then I used drugs as a teenager. Maybe *I* am the defective one," I blurt.

Tara gasps. "Defective? You think I'm defective because I lost three of our babies? How cruel can you be?" Tara jumps up from the table and starts clearing the dishes. If she slams the cupboard doors any harder, they're going to come off their hinges.

I get up and stand behind her as I take a glass from her hand. "No! You didn't listen. I don't think you're defective, I wonder if there's something wrong with me."

"Aidan, you know it's probably me. It's like karma coming back to bite me. I bet it's because I was raped. Maybe I just ruined my chances of ever being a mom."

I spin her around and gather her into a hug as I say, "Tara, you can't think that way. If you do, you give Warren Jones power over you which he just shouldn't have. Millions of couples all over the world have trouble with infertility and miscarriages."

She shrugs out of my embrace and stands in the corner of the kitchen. "I'm sorry! That's where my brain goes — I just can't help it. I'm trying to find the why in the unknowable. When Warren Jones raped me, it felt like he took away every bit of who I was as a woman away and trampled on it. I have to wonder if he took more than my virginity. What if he took my ability to be a mom?"

"They did a full work-up on you before we started fertility treatments. If Warren Jones had permanently injured you, the specialist would have found it."

"That almost makes it worse. Then it means the universe is getting back at me for being scared to be a mom. Think about it, when we first reunited, I told you I was not 'mom' material. Maybe the universe listened to me, and we'll never have the chance to be parents because I was too chicken to face up to my past."

"Tara, you had every reason to be insecure about being a mom when we first found each other again. Remember, you were almost a decade younger. We all think off-the-wall thoughts when we're growing up."

"I don't think anybody had thoughts as bizarre as mine. As a teenager, I was mad at my own mother for being unable to step up and care for me after my dad died. I possibly had one of the worst role models for motherhood ever."

"I don't argue. I was there after your dad died. I saw how much you struggled and how disconnected your mom was. That doesn't impact the kind of mom you'll be — except maybe it will make you a better mom because you know what sort of mom you don't want to be."

"What if God heard my prayers back then when I was afraid to get pregnant?"

"If God heard those prayers, he also heard our prayers when we waited month after month for the stick to have a second pink line. God wouldn't punish you for fearing what you don't know."

"I don't believe God answers prayers at all. I'm sorry, I can't believe that there is a huge, larger power out there which would allow this to happen to us."

"I know. My faith has taken a beating too. Then I remember what it took to bring us back together again after all those years. It's hard to ignore the idea that there was some overarching power making it happen."

Tara sniffs and blows her nose. "I guess."

"Yeah, there is. I can't accept the possibility that we were reunited by accident. What were the odds I would be playing at your best friend's wedding? I hadn't seen you since junior high and I had no idea where you lived. You were a famous dancer and I saw how much my brother traveled as a dancer. You could have been anywhere in the world. Yet, we ended up at the same small wedding at the same time. Someone's hand was involved."

"Okay then … God did his one good deed, but now he's gone," Tara argues.

"I don't think that's true. You could have died from blood loss during your surgery, but you didn't. I don't think we've been abandoned quite yet," I answer softly.

"So, the question is what do we do now?"

"I don't know. I wish I did, but I don't," I admit.

"Aidan, you were always the man with the answers. Don't fail me now," Tara comes back into my arms.

"I think the answer has a lot to do with how much more you can take. I can't make the decision for you. I'm not you. But, I am willing to support whatever feels right to you."

Chapter Three

Tara

"Chicken soup? Of all the soups here, you ordered me chicken soup?" I say as Heather slips a bowl of soup and a crusty baguette in front of me.

Heather shrugs. "You sounded really upset when you called a Girlfriend Posse emergency. I know when I'm upset, eating chicken soup makes me feel better."

"I appreciate the effort, but chicken soup isn't going to fix what's wrong with me." I blow on my soup.

"I know. But, it can't hurt to try. You need to eat. I know you don't want to be 'fluffy' like me, but if you lose any more weight, all your clothes are going to fall off," Heather sits down after she gives me a one-armed hug.

"I hate to make you feel like we are ganging up on you or anything, but I have to agree with Heather. I'm scared for you," Kiera adds.

I drop my gaze to the table and sigh. "I'm trying, I really am. I eat — but it's like the stress just burns it up straight away."

"I know what you mean. When we were in the middle of adopting Mindy and Rebecca, the same thing happened to me," Kiera adds with a sympathetic look.

"Rebecca? When did Becca become Rebecca?" Heather asks with a chuckle.

"I think it was right around the time her friends went from Val to Valerie and Beth to Elizabeth. I guess long names are 'in' now," Kiera responds.

"Oh no! How is Jeff taking this development? I know he doesn't like to see his kids grow up," I add.

"He says if Charlie starts to go by Charles, he's going to forbid the kids from having any more birthdays," Kiera replies with a laugh. "Jeff is such a worry-wart. He would keep them all as babies if he could."

"Do you guys ever stop worrying? I mean, it seems like every time you turn around, there is something new to fret about. How do you know what's important and what's not?"

Kiera chuckles. "Being a mom is all about on-the-job training. I worry less about Charlie than I did about Mindy and Becca, simply because I have more experience now."

"So, you felt a maternal bond with Mindy and Becca, even from the beginning?"

"Of course. Why all the questions, Tara?"

"This is really stupid — but Aidan and I have been talking. We are trying to decide what to do. I'm so lucky that I don't have to carry the financial burden of infertility treatments. Still, after all these years and three miscarriages, I don't know if I am up to trying another round of IVF."

"You know what I'm going to say," Kiera warns. "You don't have to carry a child to be a mom."

"I know that in my head, I guess — but I am the last person left in my family. If I don't have a child, it all ends with me. I know my dad would have wanted the family name to carry on."

"Mindy and Becca are every bit as much Jeff and Kiera's children as Charlie is," Heather says.

"Yeah, I know. But … I can't help feeling like I'm some sort of failure if I don't carry the child myself. This is something I started out to do, and I failed three times. Do I let infertility win?"

"I don't know if it's a win-lose proposition. Becoming a mom through adoption is every bit as real as having a child the traditional way," Kiera states.

"That's easy for you to say, you got pregnant by accident," I snap, letting my bottled up resentment of women who can have children boil over.

Kiera grimaces. "I did. And I was scared to death because of my spinal cord injury. The bottom line is all my kids are my kids. I love them all."

"I know you do. I'm not sure if I can make the same choice. I don't know if my heart is as big as yours. Maybe it's selfish, but I really want the baby to be mine. I want to be the kind of mom that my mom never was — no that's not quite true. My mom was great until my dad died. That's when it all fell apart."

"I'm sorry Tara. I wish all of this was easier. You have a huge heart. It's big enough to handle whatever decision you and Aidan make," Kiera reaches across the table and squeezes my hand in support.

"I have seen the way you work with kids. There is no way you would be able to shut your kids out of your life like your mom did to you. It just wouldn't happen. I think you can stop worrying. You've got this. Whatever the future holds, you and Aidan can handle it together." Heather hands me a Kleenex.

I can hear Aidan playing the piano as I approach our front door. This probably isn't a great sign since Aidan only plays classical music when he's stressed. I feel guilty for pushing Aidan to talk when he wasn't ready to discuss it. I ignored all the red flags.

When he sees me come through the front door, he stops playing and begins peppering me with questions, "How was lunch with the Girlfriend Posse? Did it make you feel better? Did you bring me a cookie?"

"Lunch was good as always. Yes, I brought you a cookie. I also brought you some soup if you want some," I answer, pointing at the bag at my feet.

Aidan comes over and snoops in the bag. "Oh look! It's got a happy face on it silly." He removes the cookie from the little paper bag.

I laugh at his antics. Right now, he reminds me of Mindy when she was small. Aidan loves presents just as much as my goddaughter ever did.

"I hope this means you're smiling too."

"There wasn't a cookie to explain how I feel."

"What do you mean?"

"I mean … I talked to my two best friends for a couple of hours, and I'm as confused as I ever was. I still don't know how to move forward."

Aidan sets his cookie down and pulls me into a tight hug. "I don't know if there's a right or a wrong answer to our situation. I think we simply have to muddle through and hope we find our way."

Chapter Four

Aidan

Denny pulls the dipstick out of my oil pan and wipes it off. "My daughter tells me you and Tara are having a rough time," he comments brusquely.

"Kiera's not wrong. Things have definitely been better between us in the past. This last miscarriage was tough. Much tougher than the previous ones.

"Death is never easy. The death of your hopes and dreams is equally hard."

"I didn't expect to feel so connected to this one. I guess all the checkups were going so well and we were so close to the end of Tara's first trimester, I let myself dream for a change. I couldn't feel Adriana move quite yet — in fact, I didn't even know she was a little girl until after it was all over because I asked Tara not to tell me. I wanted to be surprised. It was a horrendous way to find out."

"It's a real tragedy, for sure."

"Yeah, we were so excited. I had plans for our child.

I was going to start teaching the little one music as early as I could, and we were planning to have Tara teach our child martial arts when the time was right. I had visions of Tara teaching our daughter in her dance studio in a little pink leotard and tutu. Now that's she's gone, and I'm not sure how to stop dreaming about what could have been."

"I didn't lose Kiera when her mother became deranged from her brain tumor and threw Kiera down the stairs — but her injuries meant I had to mourn the loss of what might've been. I know it's not as extreme as what you kids have gone through, but it was still heartbreaking. It took me a long time to see Kiera in her wheelchair without remembering what it was like when she could walk, run and play like other children."

"Tara is frustrated with me because she thinks I don't feel the loss as deeply as she does. I don't know how to divide the pain between us. I can only tell you I miss the little girl I never got the opportunity to meet. I know it sounds strange, but it's true. I already imagined her starting first grade, her first recital, and her high school graduation."

"That's rough, son," Denny says as he sticks his head back under the hood of my car. "I wish there was something we could do to make it easier."

"I know. There's no manual to figure out what to do when things are broken but every time I try to talk about it with Tara, she thinks I blame her."

"Not good. Your woman takes on more blame than she has any right to. She's so stoic. Doesn't want help from anybody."

"Yeah, I thought we had pretty much worked through the whole 'stiff upper lip and don't ever tell anybody I hurt' phase." Tara was becoming like the kid she used to be back in first grade but it's like she's gone backwards. She's angry and distrustful of the world and everyone in it."

"Well, son … can you blame her?" Denny asks pointedly.

"No! That's just my point. I don't blame her for anything. The doctor said even with three miscarriages, there might not necessarily be anything specifically wrong. It may just be the world's unluckiest coincidence."

"But you don't believe them, do you?" Denny presses me.

"Honestly, I don't know what to believe," I throw my hands up in the air in frustration. "Before we got pregnant, we went to see several fertility specialists. None of them could agree on a single cause of why we weren't getting pregnant," I explain.

"I've been stuck between doctors who can't make up their minds more than once in my life."

"If they can't even explain why she was able to get pregnant in the first place, how can they explain why we lost Adriana?"

"One of the things I've learned the hard way is that medicine is both an art and science. From my point of view, the art comes into play when we decide how much to trust what they're telling us. I learned this lesson well during my wife's cancer treatment."

"We don't have any answers and it's hard to make a

choice about what to do next. I know Tara is trying to be positive but I'm reluctant to get my hopes up, I guess. Losing three makes it difficult to be hopeful. Some days I think we should give up on the whole endeavor. Maybe we weren't meant to be parents."

"Or, maybe the good Lord has a plan you haven't discovered yet. That's how it happened with Kiera and Jeff."

"I don't even know if I could recognize a plan if it hit me in the face."

"Sometimes, it's only after you're through the crisis that you realize there was a plan embedded in all the chaos," Denny says.

"Right now, it feels like there is nothing but chaos. I cannot keep putting my wife through all this pain. At some point, Tara will break. This is too much for her. I know she wants a baby, but I think the cost might just be too high."

"It sounds like at least one of you has made a decision. Are you two on the same page?"

"I don't know if we're quite there yet. I wish we were; it would make things much easier."

Denny gives me a tight smile. "Son, I've been married twice to women I considered to be the love of my life. I can tell you one thing with certainty; marriage is never truly easy. You have to work on it — especially when everything else in your world is falling apart."

"You've got that right. It does feel like my world is falling apart.

Denny shuts the hood of my car and shakes my hand. "I wish you the best of luck. Go home and remind yourself why you fell in love with your wife."

"That's the best plan I have heard in a while. Thanks for the advice.

"Don't mention it," Denny says with a little salute. "I dunno, if I were in your shoes, I might write a song or something. As my granddaughter, Mindy says, 'girls like that stuff.'

"They do indeed," I reply.

CHAPTER FIVE

TARA

I DON'T KNOW WHAT happened over at Denny's house, but my husband came back with a different attitude. For the first time in I can't remember when, Aidan invites me to go rock climbing with him. Actually, he gives me a choice between rock climbing and my favorite little backwoods bar for some line dancing.

I know it's silly. Ballet, modern dance and jazz take up my professional time, but I love a good old-fashioned line dance with a bunch of strangers. So, dancing it will be. I'm looking forward to it. It's been a while since I've looked forward to anything.

I am in the middle of getting my boots on when Aidan comes in to our bedroom. The silly man is carrying a little cellophane box with a corsage made from roses and tiny calla lilies. I look up at him with surprise. "You do realize we are going to Sawdust & Horseshoes tonight, right? This isn't some formal event — or at least I hope not. Because if it is, I'm radically underdressed."

"Don't worry, you look amazing. I just brought you

flowers to make you smile."

I take the box from him and open it. It's a wrist corsage. I hand the box back to him and say, "I think I need you to do the honors. I don't want to crush it by trying to put it over my wrist myself."

"It's my honor," Aidan responds as I offer my wrist. After he carefully places it on my wrist, he bows and kisses the back of my hand. "Are you ready to go milady?"

I place my hand on his arm as he escorts me out of the house.

As we drive toward Sawdust & Horseshoes, I ask, "What's going on? Why are we going on a date on a Thursday? Not that I object, I'm just curious about what made you change your mind. We haven't been exactly on speaking terms recently."

"That's exactly why we're going out on a date like we used to. Somehow in all the tragedy over the past eight years, we lost track of what it's like to love each other. I feel like were lurching from one bad situation to another. I don't want pain to be the entire story of our marriage."

"I don't think there's any way to avoid it. We can't stop time and pretend none of this has happened," I argue.

"No, I agree," Aidan says. "We can't avoid all the bad things, but I can respond to them better. It just occurred to me that it's been months since I did anything to remind you how amazing you are."

My eyebrows raise in surprise. "It's not just you, you know? I haven't been a joy to be around recently. It must be incredibly frustrating for you. I know it is for me. I can't figure out who I am anymore. I was supposed to be a mom, but that identity doesn't fit now. I feel like if I slide back into the person I was before I got pregnant, then I'm dishonoring my babies who didn't make it. I am afraid I might be falling back to the person I was before you and I reconnected."

"How so?" Aidan asks with a look of concern on his face.

"I'm starting to feel like I did before. Remember the days when I was afraid to leave the house? There are days, I feel like I could sink back into that place in a heartbeat. It's just easier not to deal with the outside world. I'm closing in on myself and eliminating everyone I love, including you. I don't want it to be this way."

"Have you talked to your doctor? What does she say?"

"I don't know. I haven't really said anything to her about how I'm feeling," I confess.

"She can't help you if she doesn't know what's going on."

I sigh "Yeah, I know. I'm usually a lot more proactive about this stuff. But it's hard because I've overcome so much stuff in my past. I thought I had moved beyond all the crazy mood swings."

"Tara, come on — you are being far too hard on yourself. You just went through a major trauma. We went through a trauma together. It's harder on you because you had all those hormones running around in your body and now they're gone. At least, that's what the ER doctor told me."

"You're right. It does feels like I've been hit by a car and nothing in my life will never be the same. To the world around me, nothing has changed and I'm supposed to bounce back and be the person I always was. I don't know If it's ever going to be possible. I'm just changed. I was a mother-to-be, and now I'm nothing."

"Gracie, you will never be nothing to me. You have been a part of my life for as long as I can remember. I am in love with *you* —not your ability to be a mom."

"So, you're saying we should give up?"

"No, we never give up — we just shift our focus, maybe, but I don't even know about that. I do know we have to handle it better than we have been or it will destroy us," Aidan says as he pulls into the restaurant parking lot.

He walks around the car and opens the door for me. When I get out, he gives me a gentle hug and links our fingers together in our special handshake.

"I love you too much to lose you over something like this."

"Okay. Let's work together instead of against each other. I don't plan to go anywhere. It hurts me to see you so sad." he says.

"Trust me. It hurts me too. I've never cried so much in my life."

"I'm sorry Gracie, if I could make all your pain go away, I would do it in a heartbeat. I feel helpless."

"Okay, I promise to tell Dr. Fitzgerald what's really going on. Maybe she can help."

"That sounds great. Tonight, can we just try to have

a little fun? I miss you."

"I make no guarantees, but I'll give it my best shot. After all, I always tell my students that dance is the best medicine. I should probably practice what I preach."

"Well, there you go. Dancing with me tonight is therapeutic."

"If it makes me feel better, we might have to do it a lot more often," I joke.

"Don't laugh. If dancing helps put a smile back on your face, I'd be willing to do it every day of the week and twice on Sunday."

"Somehow, I don't think you're kidding," I say as I grab his hand and walk into the restaurant.

"I'm not kidding. I'll do whatever it takes to help you feel whole again."

Chapter Six

Aidan

"Aidan, I didn't expect to see you today. What brings you by?" Kiera asks as she spins her wheelchair around and closes the door after me.

"I've got a contract I want Jeff to look over. A company wants me to endorse their products, and I want to make sure everything I want out of the deal is spelled out."

"Oh, I'm sure that won't be a problem. Unfortunately, he went over to his mom's shop to help her set up a new cash register. He should be home in a few minutes. Want to join me in the kitchen? I've got a batch of cookies in the oven."

"Really? What makes you think I would ever turn down cookies?" I grin.

I walk into the kitchen and spot Kiera and Jeff's daughter, Mindy, sitting at the breakfast bar reading a book.

She looks up at me, and her face turns pale. "Hi,

Uncle Aidan."

"Mindy Mouse! How are things?" I ask.

She frowns. "You know, I'm getting a little old for that nickname. You probably shouldn't call me that anymore."

"Technically speaking, you shouldn't call me Uncle Aidan either. I'm not your uncle and you are my employee now."

"But I'm really not an employee either; I just do gigs with you every now and then."

"That's funny. I distinctly remember signing your paycheck recently," I answer with a wink.

Mindy chews on her bottom lip for a moment before she asks, "Are you still mad at me?"

"No… I was never mad at you. Well, not since you were like eight and spilled Kool-Aid on my piano."

"So, you don't hate me?"

"Mouse, why would I hate you?"

"Because I knew what would happen to your daughter and I couldn't stop it. My gift doesn't work that way. I can't control when I see the future and when I don't —but because I didn't see it coming in time, I couldn't tell Aunt Tara to go to the hospital. If only I was better at controlling what I see and don't see, I might've made a difference."

"You can stop worrying. The doctors said that even if we would've been at the hospital, they couldn't have done anything. It was just one of those things that wasn't meant to be. It's not your fault," I say as I walk over and give her a hug.

"Are you sure? I feel so bad about it."

"Yes, we are mad at Fate, or God … whoever, but please know we have never been mad at you."

"Okay. I was really worried about that."

"However, if you have any visions about how things get better in the future, you can feel free to share."

"Aidan, you know I can't tell you that. I'm only allowed to tell you if it's a matter of life and death," Mindy answers.

I'm bothered that she was worried we were angry with her. Her gift comes with a lot of burdens, but it shouldn't make her feel like she is responsible for Tara's miscarriage. That's just too much.

While I'm lost in thought, Mindy pulls on my shirtsleeve. "Uncle Aidan, one more thing —"

"Okay," I respond as I stop in my tracks. I learned a long time ago whenever Mindy has something to say it's probably important.

"Tell Aunt Tara that better times are coming. She just needs to keep an open mind and a place in her heart."

"Mindy, if you know something, please spit it out," I beg. "Tara is on the edge right now just trying to cope with all this."

"I know Aidan. I get it. But Aunt Tara was the person who taught me the rules about using my precognition. She'd be disappointed if I made an exception for you."

I let out a heavy breath of frustration. "I know. My wife is a real stickler about the rules. I know better than to ask you to break them. I'm sorry, Mindy."

"It's okay Aidan; I know you were just grasping at straws. I'm sorry I can't help."

"Thanks for all you've done though."

"What did I do — besides make you sad?"

"Mindy, you have helped me keep my head while I was in a very bad place and keep the whole mess out of the media. I will forever owe you for that."

"That was nothing. I only wish I could've done more."

"You did all you could do. We all did. Sometimes, life doesn't have a happy ending. You're still one of my favorite pretend nieces," I remark with a smile.

"You're silly. There are only two of us and you met me first. I should be your favorite." Mindy looks at me with a sad expression and gives me one more hug before she says, "I gotta do some homework. I'll let you talk to my mom now."

As she scampers off, I can't help but think of the almost seven-year-old she was when she came into our lives. She is a lovely teenager now. I don't know where the time has gone.

Kiera puts a plate of cookies and a cup of coffee in front of me. "That was quite a conversation you had with my daughter. I knew she was sad about your loss, but I didn't realize she was blaming herself. I probably should have. It's the kind of thing Mindy is famous for."

"Yeah, I feel bad that she feels so much responsibility for the world. Tara often feels the same way if her abilities don't stop something tragic."

"How is Tara feeling now? The last time I saw her,

she was still really raw."

"She doesn't cry every day now, and the psychologist has helped her a lot. Honestly, it's helped me too. The doctor wouldn't let me off the hook."

"Has Tara become more open to the possibility of adoption?" Kiera asks.

"I think counseling is helping her understand motherhood does not necessarily require a biological connection. I don't know how to get around her family legacy issues. They are totally legitimate. I have the luxury of not having to worry about it because Rory and Renée keep having babies. My parents certainly have no shortage of grandkids."

"That's true. It takes some of the pressure off you."

"I thought she would be more open to the idea of adoption because she had a front row seat when you adopted Mindy and Becca." I take a couple of bites of my cookie.

"It's such a personal choice, it's not like you can make that decision for someone else simply because it worked for me. Of course, I am a huge proponent of adoption. My family just wouldn't be complete without my girls."

"Yeah, but remember how helpless you and Jeff felt in the beginning?"

"Boy, did we ever! It was especially hard because Becca was in the hospital."

"I wonder if Tara remembers how hard it all was for you and is afraid of going through the same thing?"

"I'm not sure. She could be,"

I nod. "Tara rarely forgets anything — ever."

"Yeah, she's kind of scary sometimes," Kiera answers with a smile but then she grows serious as she continues, "Actually, there is a reason I asked about adoption."

I raise my eyebrow in question. "Do tell —"

"A colleague told me about a family who is seeking an adoptive family for their granddaughter."

"You should have tons of people lining up for her. Babies for adoption are really scarce."

"Well, that's just the thing. The little girl is not a baby. She's almost three."

"Still, she's pretty young —"

"There's more," Kiera responds with a frown. "Madeleine is a special needs child."

I point to my cochlear implants as I challenge, "Yeah? So, what's your point?"

"The lawyers handling the adoption want to make sure the family who ends up with her can handle all of her needs. She has been in and out of Doernbecher Children's Hospital multiple times because she was a micro-preemie."

"What happened to her parents?" I ask, not able to contain my curiosity.

"Now, keep in mind I'm getting this information secondhand so I don't know how accurate it is, but it seems that the dad was never in the picture and the mom had some sort of stroke during delivery which killed her."

"Oh, wow! Poor baby. Has she been alone this whole time?"

"No, technically her grandparents have custody of her – but they are getting old and can't take care of all of her medical needs. They thought they could handle it, but after Madeleine's grandpa lost his job, they decided placement in another family might be more appropriate."

"What are they looking for in a family?" I ask, even though I know it's impulsive as heck.

"I'll be blunt here and tell you what I've heard. It might not be part of her official adoption record, but the family wants to make sure whoever ends up with Madeleine has the financial resources to take care of her and are active enough to do physical therapy with her."

"I can understand why people might think they are being shallow, but it's also smart. My parents had to declare bankruptcy after my bout of meningitis. They couldn't afford the medical bills, even with insurance."

"I knew you would understand. There are reasons I think you and Tara would be the perfect family for Madeleine. I don't know if Tara is quite ready yet."

"Neither do I. I can always ask Gracie." For the first time in months, I feel a surge of hope in my soul.

Chapter Seven

Tara

Aidan is driving me crazy. He is acting very strange and I don't know what to make of it. He's always had a ton of energy, even as a kid. He was always the class clown and disruptive in class. Until this moment, I thought he had outgrown those tendencies, but right now, he is about to climb the walls of our tent.

He finished cleaning up vocals with Tasha early, so we took off on an impromptu camping trip for a couple of days. Usually, I love the solitude and the quiet of spending time outside with Aidan. However, today there is something bizarre in the air. Aidan can barely stop moving. This made me a little nervous because he was serving as an anchor for me during a particularly slippery climb. Even so, he was hopping around like a kid who's had too much birthday cake.

The campfire is warm and inviting. Yet Aidan seems incapable of sitting down with me and enjoying it like we usually do.

Finally, I lose my patience. "Enough! I don't know

what's going on, but you are stepping on my last nerve. The therapist told us I should be very direct about what I need from you. Right now, I need you to come sit beside me and keep me warm. I'm tired of watching you bounce around like a ball in a pinball machine."

"Fair enough," Aidan says as he takes off his overcoat and drapes it around my shoulders. "I guess I'm just nervous."

"What could you possibly be nervous about?" I ask, baffled by his disclosure. "We've known each other since you were five years old. I think I know everything about you."

"I need to talk to you about something and it's hard to know where to start."

"Oh Gosh! Is there a reason you brought me out to the middle of the woods? Is it bad?"

"No! It's not bad at all. I brought you to the middle of the woods because we both love to climb and go on nature hikes."

"Then what's the problem? Just spit it out," I say as my frustration builds.

"I think I may have found our daughter," Aidan blurts.

"What are you talking about? Our daughter is dead," I growl. I have to take a deep breath to tamp down my flare of anger over his careless words.

"I'm sorry. That came out wrong. Let me back up. I was over visiting Jeff the other day to review some contract stuff. He wasn't home, so Kiera and I started talking. There is a little girl named Madeleine who is desperately looking for a home. She needs help and I think we are the family to give it to her."

"Aidan O'Brien! You cannot just go shopping for a child. That's not how it works. Look at all the hoops Jeff and Kiera had to go through to get Mindy and Becca."

"I know. But it might be different in this situation because it's a private adoption."

"Aidan, I don't know if I'm ready to commit to the adoption process. It's been less than a year since we lost Adriana."

"I know — but this little girl needs our help. Can we at least go meet her?"

"I don't even know what to say. You can't go choose a child like you choose a puppy at the pound. It's not like you can return the child if you don't like the way potty-training is going."

"I know that, Tara. But from what Kiera told me, this little girl needs a family like ours. She's currently up at Doernbecher in Portland."

"Why is she in the hospital?" I ask. Pausing for a few seconds, I add, "Wait! I don't even know if I want to know the answer. If she's sick, my heart can't handle losing another child."

"According to Kiera's friend, Madeleine isn't in any imminent danger right now. She was just born ridiculously early. She was like one of those babies you see on TV who was barely bigger than a Coke can.

"So, why is she in the hospital right now?"

"They did some sort of surgery on her hip to make it easier for her to walk. On top of that she had some sort of brain bleed when she was born and has cerebral palsy."

Sucked into the story, I press for more details, "Where are her parents?"

"I guess Madeleine's dad split." Aidan answers with a shrug.

"What a scum bucket. What about her mom?"

"Something went wrong during the delivery and she died."

"Wow! How old is this little one?"

Aidan moves his camp stool around and sits in front of me as he grasps my hands and brings them to his lips. He kisses my knuckles and cuddles my hands between his to warm them. He holds my gaze intently. "Gracie, she's three —"

"Oh, my Gosh, she's old enough to know she's alone. Please tell me someone is with her."

Aidan squeezes my hands. "Gracie, I don't know exactly. It sounds like she needs a safe, secure place to be and for all kinds of reasons, her grandparents don't feel like they can do it anymore."

"Crap! AJ, this sounds like what your parents did to you when you became deaf. Why does this keep happening?" I bat away the tears in my eyes.

"We don't have enough information to know if that's true. What I do know is they are looking for a good family for Maddie. How can we turn our back?"

"I know what it's like to be raised essentially without parents. It sucks. Still, how will I know if I can bond with her like I would with my own child?"

"I don't have the answer. I know Jeff and Kiera knew almost instantly Mindy and Becca belonged with them. They weren't even married when they started the process of adoption. We are far more stable than Kiera and Jeff were when they started."

"I don't know. Part of me wonders if it's wrong to trade a child who's alive for the one that died," I protest.

"Oh Tar," Aidan breathes. "We are not being disloyal to our daughter by opening our hearts to another child who needs us. Love doesn't come in only one size. It's as big as it needs to be."

"I suppose you're right. Do you think we could go visit her without making it all official? I just want to know how It feels to interact with her. If we don't feel a connection to her, I don't want her to be disappointed."

"Lucky for you, I'm a big star and so are you. I'll have Janine, my media gal, schedule a visit to Doernbecher. We can visit a bunch of kids and take some toys. No one will have to know our true purpose."

"That sounds like a good plan and we'll be able to make a ton of other kids happy as a bonus."

CHAPTER EIGHT

AIDAN

I've played in sold-out football arenas and not been this nervous.

"Did we forget my Gibson?" My panic starts to rise.

"No, we did not," Tara answers with an eye roll. "I have been traveling with you long enough to know we don't go anywhere without a full complement of instruments."

"By the way, you look totally hot!" I look over at Tara.

"I'm not supposed to look hot, crazy man. I'm supposed to look like an enchanted tree fairy." Tara shakes her head.

"Sure, that's what the kids will see. However, I remember you wore that outfit on the day we got engaged. I thought you were all kinds of sexy then, and I think you're even more beautiful now."

Tara blows her hair out of her eyes as she says, "That was a magical day, wasn't it? I can't believe it was so long ago. It feels like it was just yesterday."

"You know what else I remember?"

"I can't even begin to guess."

"When we worked at the day camp, I just missed out on what I thought was the opportunity of a lifetime. I was about as low as I've ever been — but, you believed I could do anything. You knew all this was coming. You had faith in me when no one else did. I don't know if I can ever thank you enough. You saved me from myself. If I'd been left to my own devices, who knows what could've happened. I was ready to give up music, but your encouragement and rock solid belief in my ability to succeed made all the difference."

"You're too talented to be held down by a dishonest production company. I was a fan then — I'm a bigger fan now. Not only are you quite literally a rock star, you manage to be ethical and kind at the same time."

"That shouldn't be so unusual that you have to point it out to me. Still, I have to agree. I'm proud of the way we run Silent Beats."

"You should be. You're one of the good guys."

"If we go forward with this, I hope whoever oversees the family selection process doesn't assume the worst about me because I am a musician. Remember the time the tabloids made all those awful assumptions about the lady on the plane just because her child had the same color of eyes as me? I don't know the best way to protect a child from all this craziness," I say, as of the enormity of the situation starts to sink in.

"Movie stars like Sandra Bullock and Nicole Kidman were able to adopt. Sandra even kept it completely away from the media until it was finalized all the way. It can be done. Your employees at Silent Beats are extremely loyal to us. I don't think they would spill anything."

"You're right. I would have to hire more security to deal with the paparazzi."

"If this is the path we choose to take, I think we can handle everything. You're good at protecting us. I have faith in you."

Although Tara made the remark in an offhand manner, it makes me give a mental sigh of relief. For the first time in a long while, she seems at peace with the idea that family comes in many forms. I know we have huge hurdles to overcome if we plan to pursue adoption, but the one I was most worried about was Tara's acceptance of the idea.

Tara has one of my tour caps pulled down over her eyes as she curls up against the door to get comfortable. "I suppose you want me to serenade you like I did on our first date?" I tease.

Tara smirks. "You can if you want, but I can't guarantee I'll be awake for it. Traveling in the car makes me sleepy and the trip to Portland is boring."

"Okay, but I have to warn you, they'll probably all be kids songs. I haven't practiced my song set for the younger fans in a very long time. I might be a little rusty."

"Rusty or not, the kids will love it. All kids love you."

"They love you too Tara. I see how your students treat you at the studio. You have as many fans as I do."

"Today, I'll settle for just one," Tara says wistfully.

———•◦———

"It sure was nice of you folks to drive all the way up here. The kids don't get many visitors this time of year because everybody is getting ready to go on vacation. Some of the teenage patients will be in seventh heaven when they figure out you are here. There may be a bulletin board or two completely dedicated to your pictures and magazine articles," the administrator gushes as he walks us through the halls.

"*We* are honored to be here." I emphasize the word we.

"Oh yes, your lovely wife has joined you. We have some dance fans here as well."

"Will most of the patients have family members here too?" Tara asks.

"Most do. Tragically there are always a few who don't for whatever reason. One of our favorite patients is alone a lot because her family members are prone to illness. They both believe exposing her to something as simple as a cold puts her health at risk because she was born so early."

"That must be difficult." I try to disguise the emotion in my voice.

"It is. The nurses try to spend a little more time with her and she's quite the little trooper."

"We have presents for all the kids, but we have

some special presents for kids who need a little extra TLC. Do me a favor and point this patient out to me when we visit her room. I'll make sure she gets one of the special ones." I point to the big backpack I'm carrying.

"That is so kind of you. I will be sure to do that. We have a deaf patient too. I am embarrassed to admit we did not arrange for an interpreter because your visit wasn't scheduled. I hope Malachi will be able to follow what's happening. I would hate for him to miss out because of our error."

Tara's face lights up. She grins widely as she says, "Don't worry about it. I've got you covered."

"You do?" The administrator says with surprise.

"Yes, Aidan and I have quite a bit of experience with American Sign Language."

The color drains from the guy's face as he stares at me. "Your name wasn't ringing any bells before — b-but I watched you on TV," he stammers. "I voted for you every single time."

"Thank you, but *America's Next Star* was a long time ago. I've moved on to bigger and better things."

"I know! One of the kids was trying to tell me you're a big star now. I didn't believe it because I thought people of your caliber usually keep to Hollywood or New York."

"I did all that earlier in my career. I decided it's best for me to stay around my friends and family and keep in touch with the real world. I didn't want to start believing my own press or anything. I'd rather not be obnoxious."

"My boss is going to kill me. We don't get very many opportunities like this, and it would've been nice to have news crews and stuff here. He likes it when high profile people come and put a spotlight on what we do here."

I straighten my back and look the guy in the eye. "I can appreciate your position, but my wife and I are here to visit the kids — not to get publicity points. Do you understand?"

"Yes, sir. Would you like me to tell the families they can't take pictures?"

"No, that's not necessary. The families can have mementos of us. I just don't want this to turn into a press junket."

"Of course, Mr. O'Brien. We don't want to take advantage of your kindness.

"It's not a problem. Let's go meet some kids."

CHAPTER NINE

TARA

I SHOULD HAVE KNOWN that Aidan would completely rock at this. He has always loved kids. We run day camps and rock climbing expeditions for hearing-impaired teenagers several times a year, and Aidan looks forward to those with great anticipation. But, his connection with these fragile children is something to behold.

Now, Aidan and Malachi are sitting on a bean bag chair playing video games. Malachi's fingers are flying as he tells Aidan about his up-coming cochlear implant surgery. He was shocked when Aidan showed off his own — complete with custom covers. In honor of our visit to the Children's Hospital, Aidan is wearing his Cookie Monster covers.

"They look like they're having a good time, the administrator comments. It's too bad I don't understand a word."

When Aidan hears the guy's question, he signs to Malachi, "Do you care if our conversation is private? Can my wife interpret?"

The little boy shrugs before he responds in sign language, "It's not like we're talking about anything private. It's only Minecraft."

When I interpret that comment for the hospital administrator, he just shakes his head and laughs softly as he says, "I always forget how typical these kids are. He sounds just like my niece."

After a few minutes, the administrator says to Malachi, "I need to let these folks visit some other kids. Thanks for entertaining the O'Briens. I really appreciate it"

When Aidan stands up to leave, Malachi hugs his knees and then signs, "You're cool."

Aidan ruffles Malachi's hair as he says, "I think you're cool too."

The next two patients visits are more like a typical fan interaction for Aidan. One girl has him sign her pic line bandage. The other requests a performance of his latest hit. At first I am puzzled about how he is going pull it off — because he usually sings it as a duet with Tasha. Aidan picks up his guitar and, before I can say anything, the teen steps right up and sings it with him as if she routinely performs with chart topping artists. When they finish, he hands a business card to the girl's mom and says, "When your daughter is well again, have her give me a call. We need some session musicians and your daughter is exceptionally talented."

I'm not sure which of them is more excited by that development. They both practically faint at the offer.

After we leave the room I hug him briefly and whisper, "You are so good. In case I forget to tell you, I love you so much. you have a big heart."

I struggle to keep my face neutral when our tour guide announces, "You mentioned you'd like to know about patients with special needs. According to the nurses, this little girl, Madeleine, spends an awful lot of time alone. I am sure she wouldn't mind a little extra attention."

When the administrator steps in front of us to walk around a gurney in the hallway, Aidan signs to me. "Are you okay? This is it."

"I'm fine," I respond quickly.

Aidan flashes me the sign for "I love you."

"The same," I sign.

I try to breathe slowly, to clear my thoughts. I am so nervous I don't even know what I want to come out of this. I have thought of little else since Aidan first told me about her. I am far too familiar with how it feels to be abandoned. Even though my dad was killed when I was young, it still felt like he abandoned me. My mom gave up on life soon after. Practically speaking, I was an orphan and I never forgot the pain. It makes my heart break for this little one.

Cautiously, we enter the room. As I grab Aidan's hand, I notice he is trembling too. It's a concrete reminder we both have a lot at stake. Aidan hides a lot of his emotions under his relaxed, affable demeanor— but it doesn't mean he is not feeling fear and pain of his own.

She's so tiny. That is my first thought as I look over at the metal crib. My heart lurches at the sight. She looks helpless as she stares at us solemnly. Her leg is in a cast all the way up to her waist. She stares at me with dark, solemn eyes. I smile and say, "Hi Madeleine, I'm Tara, and this is my husband, Aidan."

Her eyes dart over to Aidan briefly but her wary expression doesn't change.

I know that look. I wore it for many years. For a while, after my mom died, I was afraid of everything and everyone. I couldn't even leave my house.

Aidan makes his way to her bedside. She is watching his every move intently. "Hey, Maddie, do you like flowers?" Aidan asks softly.

Madeline nods ever so slightly.

Aidan smiles. "That's good because I think you might have one growing behind your ear."

Her eyes grow wide as she reaches up to touch her ear.

When she feels nothing, she shakes her head.

"Really? I'm not sure we looked carefully enough. Can I look?"

Madeleine nods her head in agreement, but she seems incredibly skeptical.

Aidan reaches out toward her and touches her head behind her ear. Magically, a little, felt daisy appears in his hand. He hands it to her with a flourish.

Madeleine blinks in disbelief — but takes the flower from Aidan. She handles it like it's made of glass as she carefully studies it from all angles. She clutches it tightly and brings it up to her nose to smell.

When she smells nothing, she offers it back to

Aidan. "It broke."

Aidan looks so *verklempt* I decide to interpret for him to make it easier for him to understand what Madeleine says.

He nods tightly at me and signs, "Thank you," as he tries to control his emotions.

Turning back toward Madeleine, he says, "Maddie, it's not broken it's made that way. It's just pretend."

Madeleine's brow furrows. "More?"

Aidan winks at me as he surreptitiously reaches into his pocket. "I don't know if you have more. I'll have to look again."

Madeleine turns her head so Aidan can reach the other ear. Aidan carefully examines her other ear and produces another flower. He theatrically sticks it behind his ear and poses.

When he moves his hair, she notices his cochlear implants. "Cookie Monster Band-Aid?" she asks as she points to Aidan's head.

"No, I don't have an owie. These are like special headphones so that I can hear."

Madeleine holds out her tiny little arm which is taped to a board of some sort. Her IV port looks huge compared to her tiny hands. "See owie?"

"I see," Aidan answers. "Does it hurt?"

Madeleine shakes her head.

I swallow hard as I pull Madeleine's present out of my bag.

"You know what makes me feel better when I have

owies?" I ask.

She just watches me intently. Abruptly she asks, "Why you a tree?"

I set the present down on her bedside table as I look down at myself. Honestly, I'm so focused on our interaction that I completely forgot I am in costume. No wonder she is a little reticent to talk to me. "I am a tree fairy today. I like to dance. Would you like to see?"

There is a spark of interest in Madeline's eyes. She smiles slightly as she nods.

Aidan walks over to the corner of the room where he set down his guitar and takes it out of the case. Madeleine watches intently as he takes a few seconds to tune the guitar. As he begins to play, she starts to sway in time with the music. I find a wide spot at the end of Madeleine's bed and start to perform a pirouette. Madeleine shrieks with delight and claps her hands. When I stop, she is grinning from ear to ear. She points to herself and asks, "Maddie dance?"

I look over at the hospital administrator and ask, "Is it okay if I hold her?"

The nurse consults Madeleine's chart for a few seconds before she says, "PT would like her to be up and out of bed more often. I don't see why you couldn't. Be careful. Her hip is a little tender."

I walk over to the head of the crib and wait for the nurse to move the railing. As I hold out my hands to Madeleine, I ask, "Would you like to dance? I'll help you."

Madeleine nods enthusiastically as she holds up her arms. I turn to the nurse. "Is there any special way I should do this?"

"She'll let you know if you do anything which hurts. Just make sure you shift positions slowly."

My nerves start to hit as the nurse talks about Madeleine's pain. I don't want to make her hurt worse. But the look of anticipation on her face is just too much. I take a deep breath and pick her up.

The first thing I notice is how light she is. I'm used to picking up Kiera and Madison's kids and the difference is remarkable.

I place my hand under her knees and clutch her to my chest. Aidan starts to play a slow melody, and I gently waltz around the room. I dip her up and down, following the rise and fall of Aidan's tune, and finish with a slow spin turn. Madeleine laughs with glee as she says, "More peas?"

I looked down at her wispy reddish-blonde hair and smile. "Certainly. I'd be glad to since you asked so nicely."

She looks over at Aidan and announces, "Maddie danced!"

I watch as my husband swallows hard and blinks away tears.

"You sure did. You look beautiful."

Aidan starts to play a country song, and I do a little line dance with Maddie in my arms. It's a good thing I know these steps by heart. I almost lose my breath when Madeleine relaxes in my arms and places her head on my shoulder. She sticks her thumb in her mouth and sighs. Aidan notices and plays a slower tune. I know enough about Aidan's songwriting style to know he is already improvising a new song.

I begin to sway gently. For several minutes, I just relish the feeling of holding a little someone as I listen to Aidan play.

"Well, will you look at that?" the nurse whispers when she checks back in on us. "She's asleep."

"I'm sorry. I didn't mean to bore her to death," I respond self-consciously.

"I'm afraid you misunderstand. It's a good thing. Madeleine is usually so fearful of outside people that she is reluctant to let the doctors or physical therapists touch her. Usually, it causes her distress. You must have the magic touch. I have never seen her this relaxed."

"Why don't you stay here with her and I'll go visit the other kids? Aidan signs to me.

"Are you sure?" I whisper.

"She needs you," he signs simply.

Aidan begins speaking again as he asks the hospital administrator, "Do we have any other kids to visit?"

"There are a few more who would love to see you. But I hate to pull you away from this," he remarks.

"Well, Tara and I are going to divide and conquer. She'll stay here until Madeleine wakes up and I'll go with you."

"That's right nice of you," he says as they head to the door. "We'll be back. I'll take good care of him."

After they leave, the nurse points to the rocking chair "You might as well have a seat. She'll get heavy after a while."

I sit down and start to rock Madeleine. She lets out a small whimper as we change positions, but then quickly snuggles closer.

For the first time, I completely understand how Kiera felt when she found Mindy at the 7-Eleven. On so many levels, holding Maddie feels like it was meant to be.

Chapter Ten

Aidan

I didn't expect the sight of my wife holding that fragile little girl to impact me so deeply. Yet, as I quietly come around the corner and see Madeleine clutching Tara's hair as she sleeps, something inside me breaks open. I am flooded with the need to make this picture my reality.

This is the portrait of my wife I knew was always there. Unfortunately, because of Tara's background, she has a difficult time seeing herself as capable of being a great mom. I know better because I watch her with the kids at the dance studio. She is so patient with them whether they are barely old enough to walk or getting ready to go off to college. She is simply amazing; she always has been.

A nurse steps in the room behind me and says, "I'm sorry to break this up, but I need to give Madeleine her medication."

Tara looks up as if she's startled to see us there. "Oh … okay. what's it for?"

The nurse smiles at Tara. "The medication will help ease her physical pain, but I think what you did today has probably been even more beneficial to her recovery. You are such a natural. You must've had lots of experience with your own kids."

Tara flinches. "Actually, I don't. So far we've been unable to have children."

"I'm so sorry. I didn't mean to speak out of turn. I figured since you reached Madeleine so easily you must be a parent. That was insensitive of me."

"It's all right. You didn't know. It's not like I advertise. Madeleine is a sweetie, though. How long do you expect her to be here? Would it be possible for us to visit again?"

"I don't mind if you come see her again, but her grandparents will need to be informed if you're specifically coming to see her."

I walk over to Tara and gently remove Madeleine from Tara's arms. I hold her against my chest for a moment before gently laying her down in the crib. Hopefully, she'll sleep deeply.

Tara digs out one of her personal cards from her purse and hands it to the nurse. "Would you please arrange for one of her grandparents to contact us? We don't want to do anything which would make them feel uncomfortable."

The nurse brightens. "Oh, this is perfect! I will pass it on to the family, and hopefully, they'll contact you.

Madeleine is clearly at home with you. I hope you get another chance to visit."

<hr>

As soon as the waitress delivers our lunch, I address the elephant in the room. "So, what did you think?" I venture carefully.

"It's funny. I've heard Jeff and Kiera tell the story of how they met and rescued the girls a million times. I didn't say anything because I am a loyal best friend, but I always questioned how they 'knew' they had to fight for Mindy and Becca. Now I find myself in the same place."

"Are you saying what I think you're saying?" I ask, trying not to sound too hopeful.

Tara smiles at me with tears in her eyes as she confirms, "Yeah, I think I am. I didn't know it was possible, but I fell in love with Madeleine almost from the second I saw her."

"She reminds me a lot of you when you first became Rory's dance partner."

"What do you mean?" Tara asks as she takes a bite of her spinach salad.

"I don't know — I guess it's her wariness."

"You know, I had the same sense about her. It's almost as if she and I are kindred spirits."

"Wariness is an accurate word. I wonder what she's been through in her life?"

"I don't really know. It's clear she adores you. She wouldn't let go of the flower you gave her."

"That was fun. The kids I usually work with are a

little too old to be impressed by magic tricks. It was a hoot to see an honest reaction by a kid who's too young to be jaded."

"Let's face it, you can charm women of all ages. You know I think you rock, but I got the impression Madeleine feels the same way."

"So, what do we do next? I want to make this happen. We are meant to be a family."

Tara sighs as she twirls the straw in her soda. "I guess we wait."

"For what?"

"For Madeleine's grandparents to contact us. I'd like a chance for us to interact again. Today was a good day, but another day might not be."

"I suck at waiting. Are you telling me there's nothing we can do? There *has* to be something."

Tara shrugs. "I'm not actually the person to ask. This is more of Kiera's area of expertise. I've heard some parents put together a scrapbook which shows them enjoying all sorts of family activities. This might make us more appealing to potential birth families."

"That makes sense. It's kind of like a visual resume."

"How do we prove we'll make good parents if we don't have any experience?"

"I'm not sure. That's probably a good question to ask Kiera."

"I'm afraid to get my hopes up. I know this sounds strange, but what if we're just setting ourselves up for a different kind of loss?"

"I know what you mean. But we can only do what we can do. Hopefully, Kiera is right, and we're exactly the kind of couple they are looking for." I reach across the table and stroke Tara's arm.

"I know. Still, I don't know if I can handle yet another disappointment. It seems like every time we get close to parenthood it all vanishes."

"Well, I've got my fingers, toes, and everything else crossed this time will be different. I hate seeing you so unhappy. It hurts my soul."

"I hope you're right. I hope this will reverse our string of bad luck," Tara answers with a grim look.

CHAPTER ELEVEN

TARA

Four days. Four very long, anxiety-filled days. That's how long it took before I got a call on my cell phone from an unknown number. I didn't use my business line for this call. I gave them my personal number which I guard like a pit bull.

"Hello," I answer after I take a deep breath. "Tara O'Brien."

"Are you a reporter?" the voice on the other end demands.

"No, I am not," I answer. "I'm not exactly a fan of them in general."

"Then tell me why you're snooping around my granddaughter's room. The girl is sick, for Pete's sake."

"Well sir, my husband and I visited several children at Doernbecher's that day."

"Did you give everyone your business card?"

I look around my kitchen and kick myself because Aidan had gone to the store for me to get some salmon. I need him right now because I don't know what to say without screwing things up. I probably should've rehearsed something with Jeff and Kiera. It didn't seem like it was going to be a big deal — but now that the moment is here and I must cope with it by myself, my nerves are threatening to take over.

I am normally a straightforward, upfront kind of person. I don't do subterfuge well. Knowing that, I decide to just state my truth. "No sir, I did not. I bonded closely with your granddaughter, and I was hoping to be able to see her again."

"You're not one of those weird pedophiles, are you?" he says skeptically.

"I can assure you I am not and neither is my husband. Let me introduce myself. My name is Tara O'Brien, and I own "The Heart Can Dance, Dance Studios. I used to be a professional ballet dancer, but now, I teach at the studio. My husband is Aidan O'Brien."

"Nice to meet you. My name is Darrell Jacobs and my wife's name is Wanda. As you saw when you met her, Madeleine is not up to dancing these days. What do you want with her?"

"I could make up some story about how I want to offer your granddaughter dance lessons to help her regain strength after her surgery, but that's just not me. So, I'm going to lay all my cards on the table."

"What are you talking about, child?" he says with an edge of frustration in his voice.

"My best friend is a social worker. Apparently, she heard from another social worker that you might be interested in finding a family for Madeleine. My husband and I are interested."

"That child is a huge responsibility. She is not well. Are you sure you could cope?"

"We are aware of Madeleine's issues and it is not a problem. We are fully capable of meeting her needs."

"As sweet as my granddaughter is, she'll never be normal," he cautions.

"We are aware of that too. I can assure you it doesn't bother us. I have a degree in Sign Language Interpreting."

"Why are you interested in my granddaughter? Wouldn't you be better off adopting a healthy newborn? Is there some reason you and your husband aren't going for a traditional adoption?"

I sigh. This isn't going very well. Unfortunately, I'm not sure how I can dig out of the hole I find myself in. Darrell Jacobs doesn't seem to like me much.

"Mr. Jacobs, I'm just going to be blunt. My husband and I recently found out — because of a very painful loss — that it's not likely I will ever be able to have my own children. We were still coming to grips with the news from the doctor when my friend told me about your granddaughter."

"Did you lose a child?" he probes.

I don't have much credibility left to squander, so I might as well tell him the whole story. He's either going to approve us or write us off as quacks. There's not much

I can do to change his impression of me at this point.

"Some people may not consider miscarriages to be real losses, but I have been pregnant three times and I'm not able to carry a baby all the way to term. To me, it feels very real."

"I'm very sorry, Mrs. O'Brien. I really am. I don't know if you heard, but we lost our daughter when Madeleine was delivered. It's the hardest thing I've ever gone through."

"I can't even imagine your level of pain —" I reply before he interrupts.

"That's part of what makes being around Madeleine so difficult. She looks just like my Erica. It's not fair. I know it's not her fault — but every time I look at her, all I can see is the child I lost. I don't know how me and the missus are going to ever get over it."

"It must be very difficult. My mother struggled with something similar. My father died when I was still in kindergarten. Apparently, I am his spitting image. It was very difficult for my mother to cope with the fact that I was still around and he was not."

"You have no idea how difficult it is for us as grandparents to resent our granddaughter for the loss of our daughter. I spend a lot of time at confession. They know me there by the sound of my footsteps."

"I'm so sorry Mr. Jacobs. That must be an awful place to be. I've been through enough in my life to know no one grieves the same. It doesn't make you evil, it doesn't even make you a bad parent. Nobody is to blame here."

"Maybe you're just being nice to me because you want to convince me to give you Madeleine. How do I know you're not one of those cat-fisher people I see on *20/20* and *Dr. Phil?*"

"You probably don't. At least not over the phone. Aidan and I are more than willing to meet you in person and you can take the measure of us for yourself."

"Do you plan to do some dog and pony show for us or will you be a regular human being we can talk to?"

"I don't even know if I could figure out how to do a dog and pony show. Aidan and I are 'what you see is what you get' kind of people."

"Okay, I'm going to give you and your husband the benefit of the doubt. We'll be up at the hospital this weekend. There is a little sandwich place nearby. It's called the Maker's Bark or Baker's Mark. I can never remember the name of the place, but my wife knows it. We'll meet you there at noon for lunch on Saturday."

"That would be so great," I reply, nearly collapsing with relief as my knees buckle.

"Be prepared. I'm planning to ask some tough questions, Missy. When I see you face-to-face, I'll be able to determine if you're feeding us a line. You can't be too careful these days — especially with children."

"I'd be disappointed if you expected any less of us." I laugh quietly before I add, "We'll be there with bells on. That's not so much of a joke. My husband takes his guitar with him everywhere he goes."

"Your husband sounds like a kick in the pants. I look forward to meeting him," he remarks. For the first time, I hear warmth in his voice. The knot in my stomach starts to ease.

"We look forward to meeting you too. Hopefully, this meeting can build a bridge between our two families."

CHAPTER TWELVE

AIDAN

"Do I look okay?" I check my teeth in the rear view mirror.

Tara studies me for a moment. "You clean up so nicely. The word handsome doesn't do you justice."

"Thank you. You look stunning yourself."

Tara looks down at the denim dress she's wearing and frowns. "I don't know if this is formal enough, but I didn't want to make it seem like we were ready to call in the lawyers either. Is there even a dress code for these situations? I always go to Heather for fashion advice, but she's at a bridal show in Eugene this weekend and can't be contacted," she frets. "Maybe I should've checked with Mindy."

"Tara, please relax. They're not going to choose us based on our clothes. There's no right or wrong outfit."

Tara sighs. "I know, you're right — but I've been overthinking this for days. Sometimes, I'm very hopeful and other times I'm scared to death they'll hate us."

"I know. I'm anxious too. I started thinking about all the dirt people can dig up on me online. I'm starting to doubt my strategy of letting the tabloids say whatever they want to about me. I figured it wouldn't matter what other people said about me because I would know the truth. Now, I wonder if I should have challenged them more. They don't make me look very good."

"There are some pretty dicey ones out there about me too. Remember the vicious reporter who decided to run a whole series of stories about how your brother was sleeping with me, claiming we've been in a secret relationship for years? I hope Darrell and Wanda are the kind of people who don't listen to the gutter-press."

I slam on the brakes as the car in front of me slows way down.

"At this rate, we might not get there in one piece," Tara says as she catches her breath.

"We're close to the hospital — the exit is right here."

"I know; I already have the directions to the sandwich bar in my phone. I've been watching the miles count down, trying not to freak out."

"I know this is hard for you, but please try to remember if it doesn't work out with Madeleine, there are lots of other children who need a home."

Tara looks at me with shock and her eyes are brimming with tears. "I don't want just any child. Madeleine and I bonded. That might not happen with another child."

"Hopefully this will go well and we won't have to

worry. I'm not ruling it out — just in case."

"Let's hope it doesn't come to that. I don't want to have to say goodbye to Madeleine. She has already worked her way into my heart."

"Mine too. Did I tell you I even had a dream about taking her fishing with Denny? It was so vivid; I woke up swearing it was real."

"I hope your dream comes true, but I'm afraid we might have gotten ahead of ourselves."

I reach out and squeeze her hand to reassure her. "Look at it this way, we'll have more answers soon. I know you'll knock their socks off just like you do with everyone else. We've got this."

⬛◆⬛

After I trade sandwich halves with Tara, I point to the plate and comment, "You should at least try to eat. We're going to have a long day and these are phenomenal."

Tara stares at the plate for a few seconds before she pushes it away, "I'll eat later. Right now, I'm too nervous to even think. My stomach feels like I've swallowed a brick."

"I know how you feel. Every time the bell jingles above the door, I hold my breath."

"You know what's funny? We have no idea what Madeleine's grandparents look like. I don't think they know what we look like either unless they've done some research. So, we have to figure out what people like Darrell and Wanda might look like."

"What if they're already here? I never even thought

about that."

"Please don't say that! Not twenty minutes ago, I was crying in front of everyone. Ugly crying would not make a very good first impression. Oh, my Gosh! I hope you're wrong."

"I'm just making conversation. We were an hour early, so I bet they won't be that early too.

"Well … Don't freak me out like that! I'm nervous enough as it is."

The bell over the front door to the restaurant chimes and an older couple walks through. They don't immediately go to the counter but instead start to search the restaurant.

I catch Gracie's eye and sign, "I bet this is it. Game faces on."

A woman walks up to us and asks, "Are you Tara O'Brien?"

For a moment, Tara freezes. I can see her warring with herself and her fear that everything will be an absolute disaster during this meeting.

Finally, she regains her composure as she says, "Yes, sorry, I'm Tara. You must be Darrell and Wanda. She politely offers her hand.

"Tara, it's an honor to meet you. Darrell is the sweetest man on the planet, but he doesn't possess much in the culture department. When he told me that you asked about Madeleine, you could've knocked me over with a feather," a woman I presume to be Wanda says as she shakes Tara's hand vigorously while she holds it between both of hers.

"No, the honor is all ours. Just treat us like you would any other couple."

"I'm sorry, I'm going to have a hard time treating you two like regular folk. You see, Erica was a huge ballet fan. She used to watch you and that other fella dance together all the time. If she could catch you on television, she would record it and play it over and over again. She wanted to perfect all of your moves."

"Wanda, I didn't get a chance to talk to you personally on the phone, but I want to tell you how sorry I am that you lost your daughter. I recently miscarried my daughter. I know it's not the same because I never had an opportunity to get to know her but, I know what loss feels like, and I wouldn't wish it on anyone."

"Nonsense. It doesn't matter how long a child has been on this earth, you will always grieve that kind of loss. I lost two before we were blessed enough to have Erica. It's not something you forget. It's something you endure."

A tear escapes from the corner of Tara's eye. "I don't know how to feel. I'm so relieved you understand, but it's horrible because it means you are part of this club that no one wants to be in."

"It's all right sweetie, I understand. It's been many years for me, and I've made my peace with it all."

Tara seems at a loss for words, so I offer, "Would you like to take a seat?"

"The manager knows where we're sitting. He'll bring our food over when it's ready."

"How does he know what you want? You didn't

have a chance to order yet," I comment in surprise.

Darrell laughs. "Well that's what you get when you're old and predictable, and you come to a restaurant as much as we do. They know us by sight here."

"Tara is that way with Panera's, they pretty much start her order as soon as they see her coming."

"See, Darrell we have something in common," Wanda observes. "They are bread and soup people like we are. This won't be so hard."

I look back and forth between them as I try to interpret the words between the words. My heart is racing as I contemplate what Wanda's words mean.

CHAPTER THIRTEEN

TARA

I WANT TO GIVE Wanda a big huge kiss. She just gave me the key to reaching them. All Aidan and I have to do is be ordinary. There's only one problem, Aidan and I have been a little spoiled by his rise to fame. Many of the things in our life aren't normal and average anymore.

As Wanda and Darrell are distracted by the arrival of their food, I sign to Aidan, "Downplay star-life."

At first, he gives me a look of befuddlement, but he finally puts together my signs so they make sense. He signs, "Okay".

Darrell turns to me and begins to speak, "I was surprised to find out you were a famous dancer."

"We are pretty normal ... really. Let me tell you a little bit about my story with Aidan. After my dad died, my mom put me in an intensive performing arts training program for dance. It was like a private school for musicians, dancers and actors. When I first met Aidan, he was just my dance partner's pesky little brother but, as Aidan and I grew up, we became the best of friends. He watched out for me even as a child."

Wanda nods as she says encouragingly, "I like a boy who was raised with manners. It speaks well of the men they become."

I smile as I replied, "That was very true about Aidan. Unfortunately, my mother also died when I was a teenager. When I came back to school, Aidan was gone."

"You didn't ditch her or anything, did you?" Daryl asks as he pins Aidan in with a skeptical glance.

"No sir, not on purpose. I contracted meningitis and I lost my hearing," Aidan responds.

"You're deaf?" Darrell sputters. "But you speak so clearly."

"My parents put me in the care of a nurse who was passionate about me not losing my speech. So, to help me cope better, we saw specialists, therapists, and audiologists — the whole nine yards. Eventually, I received these," Aidan says as he pulls back his long curly hair to reveal the implants.

"Oh! Those look … complex. Where were you at that time?" Wanda asks me.

I cringe when I have to tell her this, but I promised myself I would be honest through this process. "After my mom died, I was alone. I went through a very dark phase. It was difficult for me to interact with other people because I didn't trust their motives."

"I'm so sorry. You poor baby. So, what happened — obviously, you found Aidan again."

"I did after several years. I had done all sorts of things in my life."

"What do you mean? Nothing criminal, I hope," Darrell mutters.

"No, it wasn't illegal. I'm one of those people who really did run away to join the circus — or more precisely the fair."

"You worked the carnie circuit?" Darrell asks with surprise in his voice. My stomach sinks to my toes. I probably shouldn't have brought that up. What a stupid thing to tell them. No one wants their granddaughter raised by a former street rat.

"Yeah, I did. I was a face painter."

"Did you ever make it to the Minnesota State fair?" he asks.

"No, I never quite made it that far north."

"That's too bad, because we could've met. Until I hurt my back a few years ago, I was a carousel operator — You know the ones with horses —"

"That's impressive. At the fairs I worked at, the carousel operator is held in special esteem."

Darrell's chest puffs up as he sits straighter in his chair. "I had fourteen years in with a perfect safety record."

"That's remarkable. Congratulations!"

"Yeah, in my younger days I liked to work with the kids. But I'm just too old for that now. By the time the missus managed to carry a baby to term, we were getting on in years."

"That must be frustrating. Raising kids is tough, hard physical work."

"That's what I'm saying. To do it right, you gotta get down to their level, and run around with them and Wanda and I just can't do that anymore. That's why we're trying to find a younger family for Madeleine."

"I am so terribly sorry you have to make such a difficult decision. I want you to know if you agree to let Aidan and I adopt Madeleine, you can still be part of her life. We would not exclude you," I promise.

"Tara is right. We have no interest in shutting you out of your granddaughter's life. You would always be welcome to see her whenever you want to."

"Like one of those open adoption agreements?" Wanda asks. "I don't want to miss out of my granddaughter's life, but we wouldn't want to be in the way."

"My parents are too busy being retired and traveling to be bothered with my life, you would not be in the way," Aidan says gently.

Wanda looks at me with great sadness as she asks, "Were you never adopted after your parents passed away?"

I shake my head sadly. "No, I was already used to taking care of myself and no one noticed I was alone. Once my extended family realized my parents' estate didn't have any money, they were not interested in me."

"That's just tragic. No wonder you want to adopt Madeleine," Wanda murmurs.

"It's pretty simple," Aidan explains, in a low somber voice, "for as long as I can remember, I have always imagined us being parents. I just know she'll be a phenomenal mom. She is so talented; there's not much she can't do. We don't know why we can't have children but I can't put my wife through any more fertility treatments or the disappointment of losing yet another child. I hope you understand where I'm coming from."

Darrell takes a long drink of his coffee before he turns to Aidan and says, "Believe it or not, Wanda and I have been in your shoes. It wasn't so long before Erica came along that we were trying to adopt. It never happened because Wanda and I just don't look good on paper. I only had seasonal work which couldn't be seen as reliable, and Wanda was a self-employed hairdresser. They didn't look too kindly on our application to be parents."

"That's just so unfair," I gasp.

"You know up until Madeleine was born, I would've probably agreed with you but now I find myself on the other end of the argument and looking down on what I was. Madeleine just needs more help than we can provide. It's a lifetime commitment to raise a child with needs like hers. Wanda and I just don't have much time left," Darrell says as he squeezes Wanda's hand.

"It is so incredibly generous of you to set aside what you want to make sure that Madeleine's needs are met," Aidan says. "But Tara and I — "

"Can you hear that?" I interrupt.

"Hear what, dear?" Wanda asks looking around.

It's so rare for us to run into people who have no idea who Aidan is that it takes me off guard.

"Do you recognize this song their piping through

the restaurant?" I ask as I point to the speaker above our heads.

"I don't know what it is, but I hear it on the radio all the time. It's a catchy song."

"Thank you very much. That was the first song I ever wrote for Tara," Aidan answers.

"Are you telling me that you're the guy on the radio?" Darrell asks skeptically.

"I am," Aidan confirms. "I'm kind of proud of this one. It was nominated for a Grammy."

"Wow! I had no idea I was eating with pop star royalty," Wanda comments.

"Despite the success of my career, Tara and I lead a normal and boring life. We have lots of friends and family around to help keep us grounded."

Darrell looks over at Wanda. "Well, I guess we won't have to worry about whether our Madeleine would be taken care of. It sounds like they have the success thing well in hand."

"I need to see one more thing," Wanda warns.

"What's that?" I ask as I force the words past the lump in my throat.

"I need to see this bond between you and my granddaughter. She doesn't take to many people. I think it's because she has spent so much time in the hospital and simply doesn't know who to trust. I need to know if she trusts you," Wanda says.

"I thought you would never ask. I've been waiting for days to see Madeleine again," I respond as I stand up from the table. "Can we go right now?"

Dreams Change

"You certainly are eager," Darrell responds. "Now that I've met you, I think the two of you simply want to be parents. Let's go see how Madeleine feels about it."

Chapter Fourteen

Aidan

THERE'S A CERTAIN AMOUNT of irony to the fact that our fate is in the tiny hands of a child who is not old enough to tie her shoes.

People tend to underestimate me because of my long hair and casual laid-back demeanor. However, I care a lot more than I'm letting on.

Today is exceptionally hard because none of this is within my control. Darrell and Wanda seem to like us, but I don't know if they like us well enough to entrust their grandchild to us. Madeleine's response to us will be critical. I just hope she's having a really good day. If she doesn't remember us, or is frightened of us, it won't matter what Darrell and Wanda think of us.

The nurse who helped us a couple days ago is the one who greets us. "Oh good! You were able to get in touch. That just makes my heart so happy."

"How is Maddie today?" I clutch Tara's hand tightly.

"She just woke up from a nap. She's doing okay,

physically but she's getting restless and bored from being stuck in here with little to engage her,"

After I check the contents of my pockets, I say, "Well, let's go see if we can brighten her day."

As soon Tara and I step into the room, Madeleine smiles at us. She catches a glimpse of her grandma and grandpa. The look of confusion on her face is priceless.

Darrell steps forward. "Honey, we brought you a couple of friends to play with."

Maddie takes one look at me and says, "Flower? her gaze travels to Tara as she asks, "Tree?"

"Aww, that's precious. Hopefully, she'll be able to learn your names. Obviously, you are not Flower or Tree," Wanda says. "She is behind on her language development. That's what the doctors told us."

"To her, we represent flowers and trees. Tara was actually dressed like a tree fairy for the children a few days ago, and I gave her a felt flower — that's what Madeleine is referring to," I explain.

"I don't quite understand," Darrell replies.

"Just watch, you will—" I promise.

"Okay. I'll just sit back. I'm already impressed. Usually when Madeleine sees us, she starts to cry. I guess we remind her of physical therapy and visits to her doctors."

"That would make me a little nervous too. Kids are smart." I set my guitar down in the corner of the room. I walk over to Maddie's crib and peek in. As soon as she sees me, she grins and puts her arms out for me to pick her up.

I glance over at Darrell and Wanda as I say, "Do you mind?"

"No, by all means go ahead. Just be careful of her leg," Darrell answers.

I gingerly pick Madeleine up and balance her on my hip. With my other hand, I pretend to look in her ear. "Wow! It looks pretty clean in there. Do you think we'll find any flowers today?"

At first, Madeleine shakes her head and then she nods. Finally, she shrugs as she whispers, "Dunno."

"I don't know either, I think I'll have to look a little closer," I tease as I brush her hair out of her eyes. "Hold real still …"

Madeleine becomes a little wide-eyed statue as she waits for me to complete my magic trick.

I pull a little brightly colored felt flower from behind her ear and handed it to her. "Ta-da!"

She gives a peal of laughter and clutches the flower tightly. She turns her head the other way and asks, "More?"

"I don't know if there are any more. Let's look."

With a great deal of theatrics, I present another flower to her. She claps and then rests her head on my shoulder. "Dank you!'

She sees Tara standing in the corner, "Maddie dance?"

"Sure!" Tara offers. "I brought you a little something from my dance school. I know I always feel more like a dancer when I wear one." Tara holds out a tiny pink tutu skirt.

"Oh, isn't that the most adorable thing you've ever seen?" Wanda gushes.

I walk over to Tara and help her put it on. Fortunately, I have lots of practice at this. Rory's daughters have taken a lot of ballet lessons from Tara, so I've witnessed the challenges of putting a tutu on an excited three-year-old. As soon as I'm finished, Madeleine holds out her arms to Tara.

As Tara gets her situated, I pick up my guitar and play a couple of tunes. Tara does another modified waltz around the room. As she carefully dips Madeleine in time with the music. When it's over, Madeleine giggles and places her arms around Tara's neck. "Maddie dance more?"

I start to play a ruckus country song and Tara and Madeleine start to furiously dance. Madeleine is laughing so hard she snorts.

"Darrell, I've seen enough. Have our lawyers meet to discuss the details. If everything checks out, you will have yourself a daughter," Wanda says as she gives Tara and Madeleine a tight hug.

Darrell surreptitiously wipes his eyes as he declares, "My opinion doesn't usually count for much but I completely agree with Wanda. I think you and your wife are the missing pieces in Madeleine's life. I don't know what brought you to this spot, but I'm very glad you're here."

"A lot of things had to go right and a lot of things had to go wrong for all of us. Maybe it was because sometimes, dreams change."

EPILOGUE

TARA

I TAKE MADELEINE OUT of the walking device which allows her to hang from me like a sling and move her feet on top of my feet. It won't be long and she will be free of that device too. She's putting a lot more weight on her feet and relying on the sling much less.

I balance her on my hip as I walk over to where everyone is sitting. She reaches up and threads her hands around my neck. Madeleine kisses my cheek. "Love you, Mama."

Fighting back happy tears, I straighten her dress. Soon Aidan comes over and asks, "Do you want to come with me Maddie? Becca has some Barbie dolls to show you."

"Fine, make me do all the hard work and then you get to bribe her with Barbie dolls. There is something inherently unfair about that equation," I grumble — but I know I'm not very convincing with my large grin.

"I don't know if it's your martial arts background or your dance background, but you are much better at being her physical therapist aide than I am."

"It's not my physical training which makes a difference. You're too much of a marshmallow. She looks at you with those great big eyes and long eyelashes and you're toast. That's why you don't make a very good physical therapy aide. You have to be tough. Our daughter has thought up a million and one ways to get out of doing her therapy. I'm always amazed how much she looks like you and acts like you.   Her methods are familiar. You used to try the same thing when you were trying to get out of piano practice when we were kids."

Aidan grins. "I can't say you're wrong. Maddie is like a little mini me, right down to her red hair. *Our daughter.* Don't those two words sound magical?" Aidan says wistfully.

"They do. I can't believe all the paperwork came through today. It was like fate or something."

"I wish I could have saved you all that pain. Even so, in some ways, I think it prepared us to be better parents to Madeleine," Aidan responds trying to keep his voice even.

Receiving the final adoption papers hit me a lot harder than I expected it to. There was something truly cathartic about paperwork that declared us to be a legal parents. I look back over the past few months and I can't even remember why I was afraid that Madeleine wouldn't feel like my real daughter.

We are a real family in every way that counts.

"Don't go too far," Kiera informs Aidan as he heads off with Madeleine in his arms. "Darrell and Wanda brought cake and ice cream for Madeleine's birthday."

I groan and rub my stomach. I'm still stuffed from the barbecue."

Kiera laughs at me. "Welcome to motherhood. You need to get used to balancing being starving and not having time to eat, against all the times you have the opportunity, but have no appetite."

"I wouldn't trade it for the world. I love being a mother. Thank you for being my best friend and giving me the push I needed. I used to wonder how you could instantly fall in love with Mindy and Becca. Now, I know. Family isn't always about genetics. Sometimes, it's more about who you love."

Keira looks over at Mindy and Becca who are batting a balloon around, trying to keep it away from little Charlie. "You are totally right. I can't imagine my life without the girls. I'm so excited for you and Aidan. You guys make the perfect little family."

"You know, all those years ago when I married Aidan, he promised me he would help me find perfection. Well, it's safe to say I've found it."

Kiera reaches out to give me a hug. "I'm so glad for you. It's what we knew you deserved all along."

Darrell and Wanda walk up beside me as I am hugging Kiera. I use her wheelchair to brace myself as I stand up to meet their gaze.

"We won't be long," Darrell mumbles emotionally. "Wanda and I want to tell you how pleased we are with how you're raising Madeleine. I'm sorry I ever doubted you. I just wanted to let you know I'm happy for you guys.

If we had written a request for the ideal family for Madeleine, we couldn't have come up with a better home. Our daughter would be so happy with how things unfolded.

"Thanks for saying that. We will do our best to give Maddie the best life possible. I am happy too. I used to think I had my life all mapped out but, if it had gone to plan, we would not have adopted. For once, I am thrilled that dreams change."

"I am too," Aidan says as he balances a sleepy Madeleine on his hip.

"I'm so happy with our family, I feel like I'm dreaming while I'm still awake.

"Welcome to the Land of Perfect," Aidan says with a wink and a flourish.

I stroke Madeleine's wispy, reddish-blonde hair as I address Aidan, "I can't disagree with you. You were right … I was wrong, and I will love you every single minute of every single day for eternity.

"Let me know when you are ready for a second child," Aidan quips. "You know I'm all in. There is plenty of love to go around."

"I'll keep it in mind. If it's all the same to you, I would like this one to be out of diapers before we even think about the next."

Aiden raises an eyebrow. "But you're not ruling it out."

I shake my head. "Absolutely not. Sometimes, you just have to change the dream and make it bigger."

NOTE FROM THE AUTHOR

Dear Reader,

Thank you for taking the time to read Dreams Change. I hope you enjoyed my novella about the way love changes and grows.

The stories and the Hidden Beauty Series continue in Heart Wish where you can follow familiar characters and meet new characters from the Hidden Hearts Series in this crossover novel.

Kendall Kordes works long hours and her days are filled with the highest of highs and lowest of lows.

As much as she loves her job at Locate My Heart, an agency which helps find children, for personal reasons, it's difficult.

Her life becomes even more challenging when a ransomware attack strikes locate My Heart.

To make matters worse, the technician sent to fix the problem seems to hate her.

Jameson Payne feels justified in disliking everything Kendall and her agency stand for. But, to explain his attitude, he'll have to face some hard truths.

Can Jameson and Kendall reconcile their pasts so they can move forward?

Love should be more than just a heart wish.

You'll love this emotionally wrenching story of love lost and hope found.

Get Heart Wish in paperback, as an e-book, or for free through Kindle Unlimited.

If you would like to read more about Tara and Aidan's epic love story, they are the feature couple in So the Heart Can Dance.

Thank you,

~ *Mary*

Because love matters, differences don't.

ACKNOWLEDGEMENTS

 This book was initially part of an anthology for charity. I'd like to thank Nicole Andrews Moore for the opportunity to participate in the anthology which spurred me to write *Dreams Change*. Before she invited me, she had no idea that the prevention of premature birth was a cause so near and dear to my heart.

I have a little personal experience with the effects of being born too soon. I was born more than ten weeks early. As a result, I have spastic cerebral palsy. It impacts every second of every day. The March of Dimes does amazing work.

I would also like to thank my own adoptive parents for giving me a second chance at life. They literally saved me from institutionalization. I will be forever grateful.

I couldn't do what I do without the support of my family. Leonard, I love you for being able to see the person I really am, despite my disability.

My oldest son Brandon recently graduated from medical school. He is an osteopathic physician specializing in family medicine and we, as parents, could not be prouder of him.

Justin, you make the best eggs on the whole planet. Thank you for taking such good care of me. You are truly the master of all things egg.

Finally, I want to thank the readers for supporting fiction that tries to make a difference in the world. Without your support, we all would be nothing. Thank you for supporting my work.

About the Author

I have been lucky enough to live my own version of a romance novel. I married the guy who kissed me at summer camp. He told me on the night we met that he was going to marry me and be the father of my children.

Eventually, I stopped giggling when he said it, and we've been married for over thirty years. We have two children. The oldest is a Doctor of Osteopathy. He is across the United States completing his residency, but when he's done, he is going to come back to Oregon and practice Family Medicine. Our youngest son is now tackling high school, where he is an honor student. He is interested in becoming an EMT.

I write full time now. I have published more than thirty books and have several more underway. I volunteer my time to a variety of causes. I have worked as a Civil Rights Attorney and diversity advocate. I spent several years working for various social service agencies before becoming an attorney.

In my spare time, I love to cook, decorate cakes and, of course, I obsessively, compulsively read.

I would be honored if you would take a few moments out of your busy day to check out my website, MaryCrawfordAuthor.com. While you're there, you can sign up for my newsletter and get a free book. I will be announcing my upcoming books and giving sneak peeks as well as sponsoring giveaways and giving you information about other interesting events.

If you have questions or comments, please E-mail me at Mary@MaryCrawfordAuthor.com or find me on the following social networks:

Facebook: www.facebook.com/authormarycrawford

Website: MaryCrawfordAuthor.com

Twitter: www.twitter.com/MaryCrawfordAut

www.ingramcontent.com/pod-product-compliance
Lightning Source LLC
Chambersburg PA
CBHW032049180726
48284CB00004B/1260